The World of TENTACLE KiTTY

All rights reserved. Published by Scholastic Inc., *Publishers Since 1920.*
SCHOLASTIC and associated logos are trademarks and/or registered
trademarks of Scholastic Inc.

ISBN 978-1-338-71564-4

10 9 8 7 6 5 4 3 2   22 23 24 25 26

Printed in the U.S.A.   40

First printing 2022

Illustrations by John Merritt
Book design by Elliane Mellet and Becky James

Background photos © Shutterstock.com.

The World of TENTACLE KiTTY

by Meredith Rusu

SCHOLASTIC INC.

Greetings, Human

And welcome to a world unlike any you've ever imagined—the wonderful world of Tentacle Kitty.

We know what you're probably asking. What **IS** Tentacle Kitty?

To answer that question, you'll need to forget everything you think you know about your universe.

We'll give you a second. Take your time. Have you forgotten everything? Good. Here we go.

The Curious Story of Tentacle Kitty

Unlike what you've read in any textbook, your universe is actually made up of countless alternate dimensions. Each one is home to its own planets, creatures, and even galaxies.

Tentacle Kitty and her friends live in one of these dimensions on a planet called UnderSky, which

orbits three burning stars known as the Bright Ones. In some ways, Tentacle Kitties are a lot like Earth kittens. They like to nap, pounce on things, and they each have their own personality.

But then there's the not-so-similar stuff. Like their ten tentacles. Their insatiable appetite for Cotton Candy Mice. And their never-ending quest for **HUGS**.

But we'll get to that in a bit. For now, let's start at the beginning. The curious day Tentacle Kitty arrived on Earth . . .

The Arrival

Tentacle Kitty was just minding her own business one evening when a mysterious portal opened up in front of her and she was sucked through an interdimensional gateway toward planet Earth!

What could have caused this rip in the space-time continuum? A black hole traveling at near right angles? A sinister intergalactic enemy? Surely it couldn't have been three inexperienced

interns at the Organization research facility on Earth messing with extraterrestrial artifacts.

That last one can neither be confirmed nor denied. But one thing was for certain: Tentacle Kitty's life—and life on Earth!—would never be the same.

TOP TEN THINGS TO KNOW ABOUT
Tentacle Kitties

1. They're a lot like Earth kittens, except with ten arms.

2. Cute "kitty beans" with the texture of gecko feet run down their tentacles.

3. A group of Tentacle Kitties is called a "cuddle."

4. Their stripes appear when they're hunting Cotton Candy Mice.

5. As they grow older, they grow more tentacles.

6. A Tentacle Kitty will scratch a spot on its fur, sneeze, and that's when a new tentacle pops out!

7. Cotton Candy Mice are their favorite treat.

8. But they don't actually eat them. They just swish them around in their mouth to lick off the fluff and then spit them out.

9. They pass down the tales of their elders through storytelling.

10. They. Love. To. Hug.

MEET THE
Tentacle
Kitties

Tentacle Kitty

Always curious, always optimistic, Tentacle Kitty was the first from her planet to arrive on Earth. She took one look at humans and knew they were the purr-fect creatures to hug! It took a few tries to catch the right one. Most humans ran off screaming when they saw her wriggly tentacles reaching for them from the bushes. Weird. But when she met a human girl named Violet, it was a match made in interdimensional heaven. Now Tentacle Kitty lives with Violet in her mansion, and the two are purr-fect pals.

(As long as Violet doesn't try to give Tentacle Kitty a bath)

ALL ABOUT TENTACLE KITTY

REAL NAME: The Pink One

BIRTHDAY: December 14

FAVORITE FOOD: Grab 'n Go Cotton Candy Mice

SECRET HUGGING TACTIC: The Squeeze Play

BEST HUMAN FRIEND: Violet Love

AFRAID OF: Water. Most Tentacle Kitties are, though no one knows why.

FAVORITE DANCE: The Catwalk Shuffle

LITTLE KNOWN FACT: She shows her stripes via her Chromato-Furs.

BEAUTIFUL!!

TENTACLE KITTY SAYS

Tangles are undone
one tentacle
at a time.

Brave New World

It was an evening like any other evening. The Bright Ones were shining. The Little Ones were snoring. And Tentacle Kitty's tummy was grumbling.

She yawned and stretched her tentacles wide. "Time for a sweet treat!" she thought. And there was only one treat that would hit the spot: a sugary, fluffy, Cotton Candy Mouse.

Tentacle Kitty left her warm, cozy cuddle and crept off in search of a midnight snack. Her tentacles made little **SCHQUIP!** noises along the way. Because she was Tentacle Kitty, the sounds were super cute.

Tentacle Kitty had just caught the fluffiest Cotton Candy Mouse when, suddenly, everything turned upside down.

A gaping black portal opened in front of her, and she started to get sucked inside!

"Run, Pink One!" she heard Cat Guru, the leader of the Tentacle Kitty tribe, call.

But it was no use. Tentacle Kitty was sucked straight into the portal and zapped through to a strange new world.

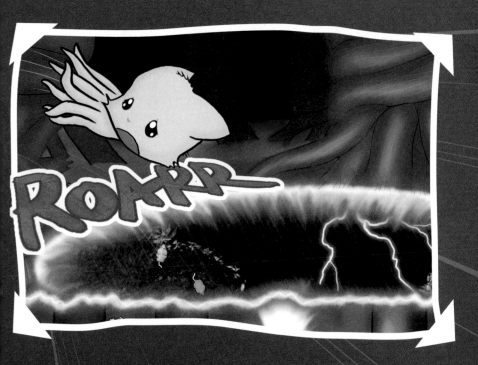

"What is this place?" Tentacle Kitty thought as she plopped down onto a hard surface surrounded by grass. Dozens of tall, furless creatures bustled this way and that. Tentacle Kitty had never seen anything like them. Each walked on two long legs. And they all seemed to be peering down at the same sort of mechanical devices with bright screens.

"Could these be the creatures Grandpa told us about?" she wondered. "The huu-mans?"

One of the creatures came running along the path toward her. Unlike the others, he wasn't looking at a small, bright screen. He seemed to just be running. For fun.

"This one looks happy!" thought Tentacle Kitty. "I'll bet he can help me. I just need to show him I'm friendly. And the best way to do that is with . . . a **HUG!**"

Tentacle Kitty schquipped directly in front of the huu-man. She stretched her tentacles wide.

The huu-man stared.

Tentacle Kitty smiled.

The huu-man blinked.

Tentacle Kitty smiled wider.

"Hug?" she asked.

"**AHHH!**" cried the huu-man. He ran in the other direction, much faster than he had been running before.

"Hmmm." Tentacle Kitty tilted her head. "It must want me to follow it."

Ninja Kitty

Cuddly by day, cunning by night. Ninja Kitty is the stealthiest cat on the planet. (At least, he thinks so.) His owner is an old man who wrote a book called *THE NINJA GUIDE TO NINJA-ING*, and Ninja Kitty learned everything he knows from it. (Fun fact: His owner read it to him.) Now Ninja Kitty hones his claw-some fighting skills in the backyard while keeping a close eye on the neighboring pets. That's how he first spotted Tentacle Kitty. He watched her come home with Violet, and he just knew she was special. Maybe it was her pink fur. Or her ten arms. Whatever it was, Ninja Kitty was a smitten kitten. He had pledged a ninja oath long ago to always be a solo cat. But the one variable he forgot about . . . was love.

ALL ABOUT NINJA KITTY

PERSONALITY: Stealthy

BIRTHDAY: November 20

FAVORITE FOOD: Sushi

SECRET CRUSH: Tentacle Kitty

FAVORITE MOVIE: *Crouching Kitty, Hidden Ninja*

WEAKNESS: Sewing (His ninja costume has no feet.)

RIVAL: Pirate Kitty

LITTLE KNOWN FACT: Ninja Kitty is wearing a mask under his ninja costume. So no one knows what his real color is.

NINJA KITTY SAYS

The greatest ninja art is the art of romance!

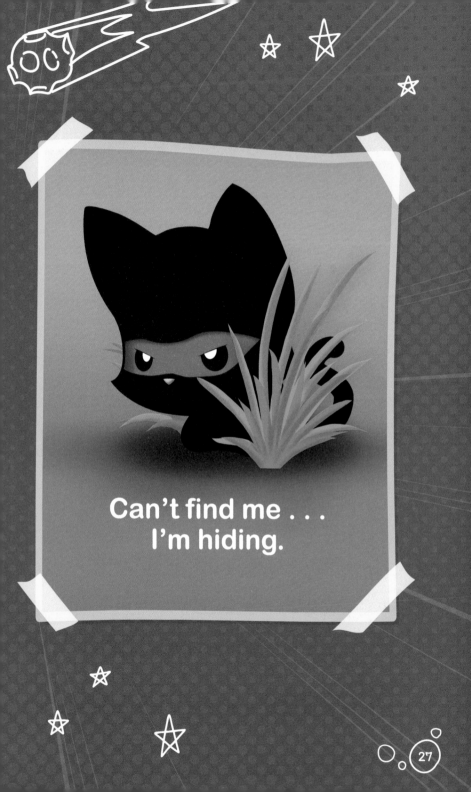

Can't find me . . .
I'm hiding.

How to Steal a Heart

It was the purr-fect plan. The stage was set. The rose petals were ready. All Ninja Kitty had to wait for was the right moment when Tentacle Kitty would walk by.

"I know I swore an oath to follow the ways of the ninja," Ninja Kitty thought to himself. "That I would never allow another kitty to steal my heart. And yet, she has. **THE PINK ONE**."

Ninja Kitty waited silently on a tree branch. Any moment now, Violet and Tentacle Kitty would walk past toward their home, and all would be revealed.

"My heart is yours, Pink One," Ninja Kitty thought. "And I will prove it!"

Ninja Kitty looked down to where a thin, nearly invisible wire stretched across the sidewalk. Rigged to the end on one side were several strategically placed shuriken with rose petals attached. As soon as Tentacle Kitty and Violet sprung the wire, the shuriken would zip forward into a tree trunk several paces in front of them, forming the shape of a heart. Ninja Kitty had clawed the words **PINK ONE + NINJA KITTY FUR-EVER** into the trunk. And once the rose petals closed around it, Tentacle Kitty would read the message and know.

"There they are!" Ninja Kitty gulped as Tentacle Kitty and Violet came up the sidewalk. "Any moment now . . ."

He held his breath. They were three steps away from the wire . . . two steps . . . one step . . . and then . . .

. . . they stepped right over it!

"Wait!" thought Ninja Kitty frantically. "That wasn't supposed to happen!"

In his frenzy, the love-smitten kitten leaped forward. But he forgot that the feet of his ninja costume were sewn together! He toppled down toward the sidewalk and hit the wire, springing the rose-petal shuriken!

"**MEOW!!!**" Ninja Kitty cried. Tentacle Kitty was right in the path of the shuriken! He had to do something!

He ninja-rolled forward at lightning speed, toppling Violet to the ground and grabbing

Tentacle Kitty into a hug, safely pushing her out of the path of the shuriken.

"Ow!" cried Violet, rubbing a bump on her head. She had no idea how close they had been to being stuck with a ninja star. "Naughty kitty! I'm going to tell your owner what you did!"

Meanwhile, Ninja Kitty was entirely tangled in Tentacle Kitty's tentacles. She blinked at him in surprise. He stared at her.

"Um . . . hi?" Tentacle Kitty said.

POOF! Ninja Kitty disappeared in a puff of ninja smoke!

"MEOW?" Tentacle Kitty asked Violet in cat language, which meant, "What was that all about?"

Violet shrugged, seeming to understand. "That ninja cat is so weird. I doubt we'll ever know."

Pirate Kitty

***M**EARRR!* Don't be askin' Pirate Kitty where he comes from, because he ain't one for sharin'. Let's just say he hails from the Isle of Yard where the sea is green and islands sprout like rosebushes. He spends most of his days aboard a full-size pirate ship in his owner's backyard. And this kitty knows everything there is to know about the swashbuckler life. He has the courage to wear a pair of pirate-themed underpants on his head as a captain's hat and a toilet paper tube for a wooden leg, so, yeah, he's **COMMITTED.** Pirate Kitty's arch nemesis is Ninja Kitty. It started over a squeaky toy vendetta. (It's better if you don't ask.) Then they realized they were both rivals in the affections for one Tentacle Kitty. Now it's an all-out claw-fest.

ALL ABOUT PIRATE KITTY

PERSONALITY: Salty

BIRTHDAY: September 19

FAVORITE FOOD: Catnip

NEVER SKIPS: Writing in his Captain's Log

TRUSTY PIRATE WEAPON: A rubber tuna

CATCH PHRASE: *Mearrr*

FIRST MATE: Squeakarr the mouse squeaky toy

FAVORITE MUSIC: A cat-tchy sea shanty

HERO: Captain Cat Sparrow

Squeakarr

PIRATE KITTY SAYS

It's the pirate life for me.

Not all treasure is
catnip and gold.

FROM THE JOURNAL OF PIRATE KITTY

CAPTAIN'S LOG, SEA DATE: 2059

It's a game of cat and mouse between me and me arch nemesis: Ninja Kitty. Not actual cat and mouse, of course. The backyard mice have taken that honor. Scurrying across me ship, leaving little surprises on the poop deck. Come to think of it, there have been more of them lately. Could have sworn some were pink and blue, and the surprises they be leaving are . . . fluffier. I told me first mate Squeakarr to keep an eye out, but, as always, I found him asleep on the job. Perhaps it's time to have another talk with him . . . on *the plank*.

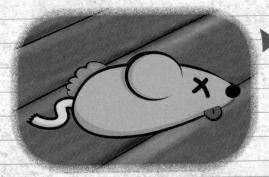

But back to the point! It's been a game of cat and mouse between Ninja Kitty and me. Dare I say, a three-sided game. For that's what it be! A love triangle between me, Ninja Kitty, and the shared object of our affection: yon Pink One.

FROM THE JOURNAL OF PIRATE KITTY

Had I but known when I first laid eyes upon yon pink lass that my love for her would be like a cutlass to my heart, I would have sailed to the farthest sea. But alas, I am struck down by adoration. And thwarted at every turn by the treacherous Ninja Kitty. The Pink One be so fair, so trusting, that she has offered her affection to the both of us, as *friends*. For her sake, Ninja Kitty and I have made an uneasy truce.

But in reality, it is all a ruse! Ninja Kitty
knows neither the time, nor the place.
But when he least expects it, he will
get what's coming to him, and Tentacle
Kitty will see once and
for all that I am the
true warrior who
deserves her
affection.

I would write
more, but I
trust not even
my Captain's
Log to keep true the
secrets of my heart. Until
next time. Stay brave. Sail true. And
always aim for the cat's eye of glory.

Cotton Candy Mice

When Tentacle Kitty traveled to Earth, she wasn't alone. Dozens of Cotton Candy Mice accidently tumbled through the portal with her. These colorful vermin eat sugar-crystal plants on UnderSky, making their fluff taste like cotton candy. Here on Earth, they've discovered sugar abounds in dumpsters. It didn't take long for them to eat. And multiply. So, no, that colorful piece of fluff waddling down the sidewalk isn't a piece of carnival treat. It is a rodent. From another dimension. And they will double in number by tomorrow.

Cotton Candy Mouse fluff is a favorite snack of Tentacle Kitties on UnderSky, but if a human were to eat the fluff (because, hey, cotton candy!), they would get the worst stomachache ever and wind up walking around like a zombie for twenty-four hours. But don't worry, they don't bite. Humans just drool and moan a lot. Talk about a mousetrap.

ALL ABOUT COTTON CANDY MICE

PERSONALITY: Skittish

LIKES: Sugar

DISLIKES: Rain

KNOWN COLORS: Pink and blue

DEFENSE TACTIC: Staying really still so no one notices them. If that fails, fainting.

LITTLE KNOWN FACT: Their skin color matches their fluff.

GOOD AT: Multiplying

While the Cat's Away

A Cotton Candy Mouse Collection of Nursery Rhymes

Hickory, dickory, dock.

The Cotton Candy Mouse

ran up the clock.

But it was a trick.

And then it got licked!

Hickory, dickory, dock.

Three candy mice.

See how they run.

Toward the carnival filled with sweets.

Everyone thought they were the treats.

And now the people have zombie feet!

Three candy mice.

Rat Tailed Unicorns

Don't be fooled by these unicorn-ish creatures' mystical appearance. They are really invasive pests from another dimension. No one knows exactly where they came from. They just showed up one night, staring at all the suburban Earth lawns with their creepy eyes. That's when *it* started. The Glitterings.

A Rat Tailed Unicorn's favorite activity is sneezing glitter All. Over. Your. Property. The glitter takes months to wash away and your grass will never look the same. They're also experts at poking holes in foundations with their horns and collecting bits of metal from stop signs and traffic lights for their hives. Nocturnal by nature, these peculiar pests close their eyes during the day and hum eerie tunes as echolocation. But as soon as night falls, that's when they open their eyes and stare into your soul. They're not dangerous . . . per se. But no one can *un*-see something that creepy.

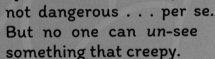

ALL ABOUT RAT TAILED UNICORNS

PERSONALITY: Conformists. They have a hive mentality.

FUN FACT: They have a queen. Great.

SNEEZES: Ultra-fine 0.008-inch hexagonal glitter

FAVORITE PASTIME: Poking holes in valuable things

LIKES: The night

DISLIKES: Off-key flutes

FAVORITE FOOD: Your hair

HOME PLANET: ???

RAT TAILED UNICORN SAYS

The darker the night,
the brighter the glitter.

Watch where you step.
Don't worry. I fixed your
drainage problem.

The Glittering

What is that?

Dad, I'm scared.

It's okay. I'm sure it's just a pony . . . or something.

The Little Ones

Young Tentacle Kitties are called Little Ones. With their bright colors and lovable eyes, they're all-around precious. Little Ones like playing with flowers, rolling in grass, and sticking their tentacle suction cups onto tree bark just to hear the adorable *SCHQUIP!* noises they make.

They'll pretend to be brave as they venture off in search of Cotton Candy Mice, but they never stray too far from home. They look up to their caretaker, Cat Guru, to keep them safe. Cat Guru has a habit of teasing them with scary bedtime stories or bad grandpa jokes. But the Little Ones don't mind. If the scary stories keep them up at night, they just wake Cat Guru so they can snuggle together and feel safe. Now **THAT'S** a true cuddle.

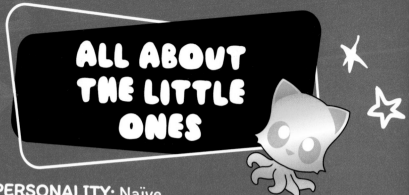

ALL ABOUT THE LITTLE ONES

PERSONALITY: Naïve

LIKES: Naps in the sunlight

DISLIKES: Scary stories

FAVORITE PASTIMES: Eating, sleeping, and playing

PRACTICES: Roaring to startle Cotton Candy Mice

SECRET WEAPON: Cuteness overload

WOULD NEVER: Venture too far away from the cuddle

FUN FACT: During fur-shedding season, their multicolored fur mixes together to make rainbow fluffballs.

BEWARE THE CUTENESS

Cat Guru

Cat Guru, or "Grandpa" as Tentacle Kitty calls him, is the elder of Tentacle Kitty's species. This sage leader is masterful at passing down the knowledge of their tribe through storytelling. One of his favorite pastimes is freaking out the Little Ones with spooky stories of weird interdimensional beings. But he only teases them because he likes looking after them so much. Cat Guru has a wealth of wisdom, and he actually spent some time with humans when he was young, so he knows all about Earth and its people. Tentacle Kitty has learned about humans from his stories, and thanks to him, she wasn't fully unprepared when she landed on our planet.

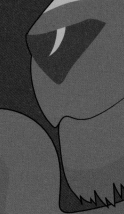

ALL ABOUT CAT GURU

PERSONALITY: Wise and a little cantankerous

BIRTHDAY: February 34

FAVORITE FOOD: Fluffernutters

KNOWN FOR: His storytelling skills

WEIRD FACT: He was the runt of the litter when he was born, but then he grew huge.

DISTINGUISHING FEATURE: He has fewer tentacles than most elders.

STRENGTH: His vast knowledge

WEAKNESS: He has terrible allergies.

CAT GURU SAYS

All that glitters is not gold.
It's likely a Rat Tailed
Unicorn sneeze.

A Tentacle Kitty's strength
comes not from knowledge,
but knowledge shared.

Violet Love

Violet Love was Tentacle Kitty's first friend on Earth. Unlike other humans, Violet wasn't weirded out by Tentacle Kitty's tentacles. She thought the Pink One was adorable! Perhaps that's because so much of what Violet is used to is what others would call . . . unusual. She lives in an old Victorian house with a robot butler named Howie, and no one knows for certain when her mom and dad will be back. But Violet is smart, self-sufficient, and determined to hold down the fort until their return. She can be a little awkward around other people, especially when she starts talking about her favorite manga or the latest cosplay convention. But if there was anyone who was born ready to handle the interdimensional adventures that come with a Tentacle Kitty, it was Violet.

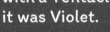

ALL ABOUT VIOLET

PERSONALITY: Happy and a bit geeky

BIRTHDAY: November 7

LIKES: Video games and anime

DISLIKES: Feeling left out

STRENGTHS: She's super smart.

DEFINING FEATURE: Purple streak in her hair

FUN FACT: Her house is down the road from Pirate Kitty's and Ninja Kitty's houses, making her yard a sort of neutral zone.

PRIZED POSSESSION: A heart-shaped necklace that has a secret ability . . .

Eat. Love. Play.

You can't have a rainbow
without a little rain.

Clocksworth

Clocksworth is an automaton from unknown origins who just happens to live in the very ship grounded in Pirate Kitty's backyard. Tentacle Kitty and her friends were shocked when they discovered him. He explained that the ship was never meant to sail the seven seas. It's really an interdimensional vessel that crash-landed on Earth years ago, and Clocksworth is the captain! He's the only one who knows how to make it work, but as long as he's at the helm, everything is under control. Sort of. Just never forget to respect teatime. Tea is Clocksworth's passion, and according to him, there's nothing a spot of tea can't fix. Sprained ankle? Darjeeling! Run out of fuel? Earl Grey! This often doesn't help in sticky situations. But since he speaks with a proper British accent, it feels like what he's saying must be true.

ALL ABOUT CLOCKSWORTH

PERSONALITY: Dignified

BIRTHDAY: Unknown. But it's probable he was built on the Queen's birthday.

LIKES: Tea

DISLIKES: Running out of tea. (It's a crisis, really.)

DEFINING FEATURES: A top hat built into his head; a flat metal mustache; and a monocle, which is actually his eye and can be detached to look around corners

FUN FACT: His six tentacles retract into his hat when he sleeps.

PRIZED POSSESSION: His giant vault of teas from multiple dimensions

SECRET: He has a hidden stash of Emergen-tea somewhere aboard *Levia*, the interdimensional ship.

CLOCKSWORTH SAYS

For a relaxing time,
make it teatime.

To Infini-tea and Beyond!

Levia

*L*evia (pronounced like "papaya") looked like just an ordinary pirate ship half-buried in a suburban backyard. Because you know, that's normal. But she's actually a living spaceship that can travel through dimensions. She can also shape-shift to blend into her surroundings, mirroring anything from clown cars and skyscrapers to windmills and poodles. Her shape-shifting skills get a little muddled when she's stressed. (Like the time she ran out of fuel and crash-landed on Earth because Clocksworth was so distracted because his tea supply was low.) So that's how she ended up looking like a pirate ship in Pirate Kitty's backyard in the first place.

But when she's feeling calm, *Levia*'s preferred form is a whale. *Levia* was stuck in Pirate Kitty's backyard until Violet's heart necklace mysteriously activated her. Now that she's up and running again, there's no telling what dimension they'll head to next!

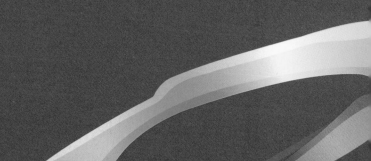

ALL ABOUT LEVIA

PERSONALITY: Ambiguous

BIRTHDAY: ???

SPECIES: Mirage

ORIGINAL SHAPE: Unknown. She picked a whale because she thinks they're pretty.

BEST FRIEND: Clocksworth. They're like tea and honey!

LIKES: Dimension diving

DISLIKES: Confusion

SECRET WISH: To find another shapeshifter like herself. She hasn't seen another member of her species in a very long time.

Levia Schematic

← ∞ **Tea Cupboard**
(Seems to go on forever!!)

? ? ?

Tea Room

Levia is a mysterious creature! She seems to be able to make rooms wherever and whenever her friends need them!

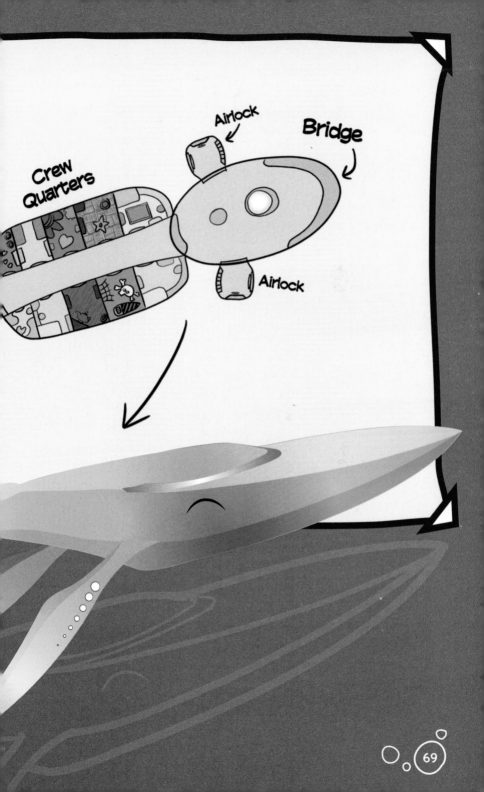

Crew Quarters

Airlock

Bridge

Airlock

THE WONDERFUL WORLD(S) OF
Tentacle Kitty

Every day with Tentacle Kitty is a new adventure, whether she's exploring UnderSky, the Milky Way, or beyond!

UnderSky Adventures

CHASING COTTON CANDY MICE

Sugar high and feline fine!

Earthbound Adventures

THE NEVER-ENDING QUEST FOR HUGS

I should hug one before it sees me.

AAAAAHHH

Well, that didn't work . . .

Maybe if I slow it down a little.

EEP

A AAAHH

EEEEE

. . . I'm starting to think they are scared . . .

Too slow maybe?

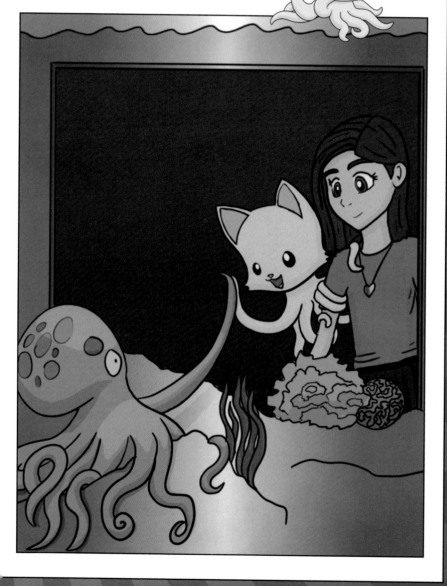

MAKING NEW FRIENDS

Sharpening Ninja Skills

YOU WON'T ESCAPE THIS TIME!

YOU ARE NO MATCH FOR NINJA KITTY!

Living the Pirate Life

Interdimensional Adventures

Tentacle Kitty
DOs and DON'Ts

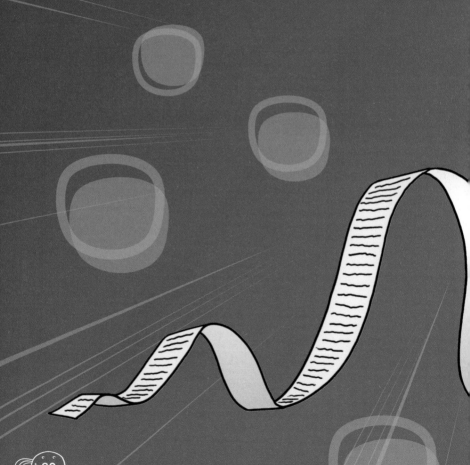

DON'T:

Go in the water.
You never know what
might be lurking in there.

Believe in the impossible.

DON'T:

Trip over your own two feet.

Enjoy the finer things in life.

DON'T:

Eat food off the ground. You never know where it's been . . . or what it might be.

KEEP
CALM
AND
HUG
EVERYONE

Fun and Games

Tentacle Kitty's
Comedy Cuddle

Q: What do you call twin Little Ones?

A: I-tentacle

Q: What did the Rat Tailed Unicorn buy at the market?

A: Hole foods

Q: What's Ninja Kitty's favorite weapon?

A: Cat-tanas

Q: What's Clocksworth's favorite letter?

A: T

Q: Why didn't the Little One want to eat the clown Cotton Candy Mouse?

A: It tasted funny.

Q: What does Clocksworth call early morning teatime?

A: After-moon tea

Q: Can Ninja Kitty see Pirate Kitty in the dark?

A: Shuriken!

Q: What's Pirate Kitty's favorite type of exercise?

A: The plank

Q: Why do the Little Ones always get their way?

A: They're very purr-suasive.

Q: Why didn't Tentacle Kitty want to eat lemons?

A: She didn't want to be a sourpuss.

Q: What would you call Levia if she shape-shifted into an insect?

A: Le-fly-a

Riddle Tea This

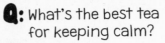

Q: What's the best tea for keeping calm?

A: Sereni-tea

Q: Which tea is best for handling delicate situations?

A: Ginger tea

Q: Which tea do you drink to stay healthy?

A: Immuni-tea

Q: What did one green tea say to the other?

A: Pleased to matcha.

Q: What did the viscount and the marquess get when they mixed black and white tea?

A: Earl grey

Q: Which tea helps boost your mood?

A: Positivi-tea

Q: What's a ghost's favorite tea?

A: Boo-long

Q: Why does Clocksworth always win at tea auctions?

A: He's not afraid of paying a steep price.

A List of Teas from
Clocksworth's Vault

EMERGEN-TEA:
In case of emergency, brew this.

KOALA-TEA:
Better than the average brew

GOAT-TEA:
When you need a quick disguise

BOAT-TEA:
McBoat Taste

CON-TEA-PLATION:
Great for letting your mind Simmer

PAR-TEA:
Celebrate Brew Times!

TRANQUILI-TEA:
When you need to find your zen

CREATIVI-TEA:
A dip of this, a dash of that, mix it together and look at that

ROYAL-TEA:
Exclusively for the most prestigious guests

FLIRT-TEA:
When you need to break the ice, try something hot.

SALT-TEA:
BLECH! I thought it was sugar!

GRAVI-TEA:
Keeps you grounded

SAFE-TEA:
It's more fun when you come home in one piece.

FEIS-TEA:
MEARRR! (Pirate Kitty Sipping it)

FORMALI-TEA:
Always lift your pinky.

Tentacles of Knowledge

You miss 100 percent of the Cotton Candy Mice you don't chase.

Nap like no one is watching.

Squeeze the most out of life.

I think, therefore *MEARRR!*

The journey through a thousand dimensions begins with one dimension dive.

A stranger is just a friend you haven't hugged yet.

See You Out There!

It's a brave new world for Tentacle Kitty and her friends, and the adventure is just beginning! But as long as these unlikely companions have one another, they know anything is possible. Until next time, stay pawsitive. And keep an eye out. You never know when a portal might open in your backyard and *Levia* will pop through. If she does, you're welcome aboard! Cotton Candy Mice are welcome, too. Just promise you won't bring any Rat Tailed Unicorns along for the ride.